Club

For Princess Penny,
because she likes the baby dragon.
With much love and many thanks, xx
VF

For my darling
Olly x
SG

www.tiaraclub.co.uk

ORCHARD BOOKS
338 Euston Road, London NW1 3BH
Orchard Books Australia
Hachette Children's Books
Level 17/207 Kent Street, Sydney, NSW 2000, Australia
A Paperback Original
First published in Great Britain in 2005
Text © Vivian French 2005
Illustrations © Sarah Gibb 2005
The rights of Vivian French and Sarah Gibb to be
identified as the author and illustrator of this work
have been asserted by them in accordance with
the Copyright, Designs and Patents Act, 1988.

A CIP catalogue record for this book is available
from the British Library.
ISBN 1 84362 864 3
3 5 7 9 10 8 6 4

Printed in Great Britain

The Tiara Club

Princess Daisy
and the Dazzling Dragon

By Vivian French
Illustrated by Sarah Gibb

ORCHARD BOOKS

The Royal Palace Academy
for the Preparation of Perfect Princesses

(Known to our students as '*The Princess Academy*')

OUR SCHOOL MOTTO:

*A Perfect Princess always thinks of others before herself,
and is kind, caring and truthful.*

We offer the complete curriculum for all princesses, including –

*How to talk
to a Dragon*

*Designing and Creating
the Perfect Ball Gown*

*Creative Cooking for
Perfect Palace Parties*

*Avoiding Magical
Mistakes*

*Wishes, and how
to use them Wisely*

*Descending a Staircase
as if Floating on Air*

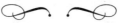

Our head teacher, Queen Gloriana, is present at all times, and students are well looked after by the school Fairy Godmother.

Visiting tutors and experts include –

KING PERCIVAL
(Dragons)

QUEEN MOTHER MATILDA
(Etiquette, Posture and Poise)

LADY VICTORIA
(Banquets)

THE GRAND HIGH DUCHESS
DELIA *(Costume)*

We award tiara points to encourage
our princesses towards the next level.
All princesses who win enough points in their
first year are welcomed to the Tiara Club
and presented with a silver tiara.

Tiara Club princesses are invited to return
next year to Silver Towers, our very special
residence for Perfect Princesses, where
they may continue their education
at a higher level.

PLEASE NOTE:
Princesses are expected to arrive at the Academy
with a *minimum* of:

TWENTY BALL GOWNS
(with all necessary hoops,
petticoats, etc)

TWELVE DAY DRESSES

SEVEN GOWNS
suitable for garden parties,
and other special
day occasions

TWELVE TIARAS

DANCING SHOES
five pairs

VELVET SLIPPERS
three pairs

RIDING BOOTS
two pairs

Cloaks, muffs, stoles, gloves
and other essential
accessories as required

Hello! And I SO want to say hello to you properly. Should I say, "Good day Your Majesty?" That doesn't sound very friendly, and I DO want us to be friends! After all, we're at the Princess Academy together, aren't we? Ooops! I nearly forgot to tell you I'm Daisy! Princess Daisy. Have you met my other friends - Charlotte, Katie, Alice, Emily and Sophia? They're learning to be Perfect Princesses, just like you and me. It's fun most of the time, but Princess Perfecta isn't very nice. We're really REALLY happy that she doesn't share the Rose Room dormitory with us. She's much too horrid!

Chapter One

Do you ever get scared of things?
I do. For one thing, I'm scared I'll
NEVER get five hundred tiara
points by the end of my first year
here at the Academy, and then I
won't be allowed to join the Tiara
Club – and I DO so want to! It
sounds SO wonderful! And I'm
scared of things like spiders, and

big fierce dogs. Actually, thinking about ANYTHING big and fierce makes my knees wobble! Our head teacher, Queen Gloriana, is scary too. She's very tall and gracious, but she can look SO fierce if you do something wrong. Fairy G is much friendlier, but even she can get angry, and when she does she swells up to TWICE her usual size. Honestly! I'm not joking!

When I first heard we were going to meet a real dragon, I was SO frightened I got hiccups. We were having breakfast, and Queen Gloriana and Fairy

Godmother came in to say good morning.

"Good morning, my dear young princesses," Queen Gloriana said.

"Now, I have a very important announcement for the first year students. This morning, as you know, you have *Creative Cake Cooking for Perfect Palace Parties*. This afternoon, however, you are to go straight to the Tower Room just as soon as you've finished lunch. You are MOST fortunate; King Percival has agreed to bring in one of his dragons!"

You could have heard a pin drop. My heart was beating so fast I thought I might burst, and then I hiccupped. I was SO embarrassed!

"Now," our head teacher went on, "I want you all to listen very carefully to what King Percival tells you. He will be instructing you on *How to Talk to Dragons*, and he will give you your tiara points at the end of the lesson. I look forward to hearing that you all have at LEAST ten points!" And then she swept out of the dining hall, and Fairy G – who is MUCH too huge to sweep – stamped after her.

Of course we all started to talk at once, except for Princess Perfecta and Princess Floreen. Perfecta pretended to give a bored yawn, and Floreen immediately copied her. Just because Perfecta was at the Academy last year she thinks she knows EVERYTHING, even though she only got about a hundred tiara points in the whole year! Alice's sister said Queen Gloriana was FURIOUS with her, and now she's back in the first year with us.

"A DRAGON!" Katie said, and her eyes were shining. "What FUN!"

"Do you think it'll be VERY big?" I asked nervously.

"HUGE and FEROCIOUS!" Charlotte said, but Princess Sophia shook her head. "Queen Gloriana would never allow that," she said. "I expect it'll be a

very old dragon that can't even breathe fire any more."

"Come on!" Alice stood up. "Let's go and get boring old Cake Cookery over. Then we can see the dragon for real! Hurry up and finish your toast, Daisy."

I looked at the toast lying untouched on my plate. I didn't feel very hungry...especially when I saw the burnt edges. They made me think of fiery breath.

"I've finished, thank you," I said.

Emily took my hand as we hurried out of the dining room. "Don't worry," she whispered. "It'll be OK. At least, I hope so!"

Behind us Princess Perfecta said loudly, "Some people are SUCH scaredy cats!"

Chapter Two

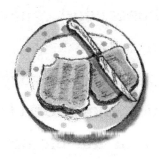

Our cooking lesson was a DISASTER! Usually I quite enjoy it, because when I'm at home our cook won't let me near the kitchen. She says it's Not The Place For Princesses, and chases me away with a big wooden spoon. Luckily Queen Gloriana thinks we should know how to cook just in case we don't live Happily Ever After. Also she says that some Royal Families are really poor, and can't afford cooks.

Anyway, I was so busy worrying about the dragon that I didn't listen when Lady Victoria told us what temperature we should set the oven to. My fairy cakes came out TOTALLY black.

Floreen said loudly, "Who needs the fire brigade, then?" and she and Perfecta sniggered together.

"Take no notice of her," Sophia said. "Here – you can have some of mine!"

Katie looked at my baking tray and giggled. "They look like lumps of coal!" she said. "Throw them away quickly before Lady V sees them – she'll have a fit!"

Katie was quite right. They did look like coal, and I couldn't help giggling myself as I looked round for the bin. I couldn't see it, so I dropped my poor little cakes into my school bag just as Lady V tippy-toed over to us. (She wears SUCH high heels!)

We tried to look innocent as Lady V peered over her glasses at our baking trays.

"Not QUITE as lovely as I'd hoped," she said. "Daisy dear, let me try yours!" She picked up one of my cakes (of course, it was really one of Sophia's) and nibbled at it.

"Oh NO!" she exclaimed. "SALT instead of sugar! Oh dear me. I can't give a single one of you any tiara points. WHAT disappointing little cooks you are!

I was SO hoping your fairy cakes would be the pride of King Percival's Celebration Party tonight."

Floreen sat up at once. You could almost see her ears flapping. "A PARTY, Lady Victoria?"

Lady V waved a dismissive hand. "For King Percival's SPECIAL friends only, Princess Floreen. Lots of fireworks, and dancing in the moonlight in the roof garden of his wonderful crystal tower." She looked at us sadly. "I'd planned to present him with a mountain of fairy cakes iced with pearly pink icing."

"Please, Lady Victoria – my fairy cakes are LOVELY!" Perfecta called out, and under her breath she muttered, "and I didn't cheat like scaredy cat Daisy!"

Lady V shook her head. "No, Perfecta dear. Yours are a teensy bit undercooked. And please take

two MINUS tiara points for calling out so boastfully."

Perfecta scowled as Lady V tippy-toed away. Then the bell rang loudly, and we all trooped out into the corridor and headed for lunch.

I couldn't eat any of my pizza. I kept thinking I could smell smoke, and it made me twitchy. Emily didn't eat much either.

"The dragon will be on a chain, won't it?" she asked Alice.

Alice rubbed her nose. "I don't know. When my big sister was here she never met a real dragon. King Percival was supposed to bring one in, but she was ill, or having a baby or something, and he brought in a cardboard cut-out one instead. My sis was REALLY fed up!"

"Oh," Emily said in a very small voice.

Knowing Emily was anxious made me feel a bit braver. "We'll keep together," I said.

"Scaredy cats!" hissed Floreen, and Perfecta laughed.

"We'll ALL stay together," Sophia said firmly.

Emily and I held hands tightly as we tiptoed up the stairs towards the tower room. Usually it's my favourite room – it's got a HUGE window that opens on to the Academy roof, and you can see for miles and miles and miles – but this time I went up the stairs REALLY slowly.

Sophia and Alice were holding hands as well, and even Charlotte and Katie hesitated before they went through the doorway.

"Oooooh!" I quavered. "I'm scared, Emily!"

"Me too," Emily said, and her voice was shaking. "But we ARE princesses..."

I swallowed hard. "Yes," I said. "Let's go!"

And in we went, expecting to see a HUGE dragon with glittering scales and ferocious glaring eyes. I was all ready to run away if it was too dreadful...

...but it wasn't dreadful at all.

The dragon was totally GORGEOUS!

Chapter Three

Alice, Katie, Sophia and Charlotte and the rest of the first year princesses were already making little "Ooooh!" and "Aaaah!" noises, and I could SO see why. It was just a baby, with shimmery scales on its fat silver tummy, and the sweetest tiny green wings.

33

It was gazing at us with huge golden eyes, and it truly looked as if the poor little thing was scared of US!

King Percival was standing behind the little dragon, and he was actually smiling! King P's about a hundred years old, and very fat and whiskery, and normally he frowns a lot...especially when we get things wrong in the classes where he teaches us how to be Polite to Princes (we are SO not good at that!) But this time he was looking really pleased and proud.

"HA!" he said. "Jolly little beast, isn't he? Gotta get him trained, of course, but he's doing fine. Want to tickle his ears?

Sort of thing you girls like doing, after all. Good introduction to dragons, too. You'll never be afraid of the big ones once you've met a little one."

I could see Katie's eyes sparkle. "Can we really?" she asked. "He's SO beautiful."

King P puffed out his stomach, just as if HE was the proud father. "Suppose he IS a bit of a stunner," he said. "Now, move slowly. Don't want to give him a fright."

Katie and Charlotte tiptoed towards the little dragon, and while Katie tickled his ears Charlotte scratched him under his chin. He made a funny little purring noise, and you could SO see he liked it.

"Good girls!" King P said.

"Glad to see you're not afraid of the little chap. Next!"

He looked straight at me, but before I could say ANYTHING Perfecta put up her hand.

"You'll have to excuse Princess Daisy, Your Majesty," she said in a horrible sneery voice. "She's PETRIFIED of dragons!"

"No, I'm NOT!" I said. I was FURIOUS! That little dragon was so cute I was DYING to give him a cuddle. I glared at Perfecta and took a BIG step forward, and at exactly that moment Floreen put out her foot. I tripped, and fell with a HUGE crash.

The dragon let out a wail and dashed for the window – and before any of us could move he'd smashed through the glass and was scampering about on the flat bit of the roof outside.

And then the MOST incredibly scary thing happened! There was a HUMUNGOUS ROAR, and a GIANT puff of smoke – and the most enormous dragon you could ever imagine came flying up from somewhere down below. Her scales glittered and shone, and as she turned and twisted in the air her massive leathery wings beat up and down with a

THWUMP! THWUMP! sound. Her huge golden eyes were angry, and as we stood totally frozen to the floor a blast of flame shot across the broken window.

We could actually hear the glass sizzling as it melted!

And then King Percival did something INCREDIBLY brave. He ran straight towards the gaping hole where the red hot glass was still dripping, and began blowing and blowing on a silver whistle round his neck...

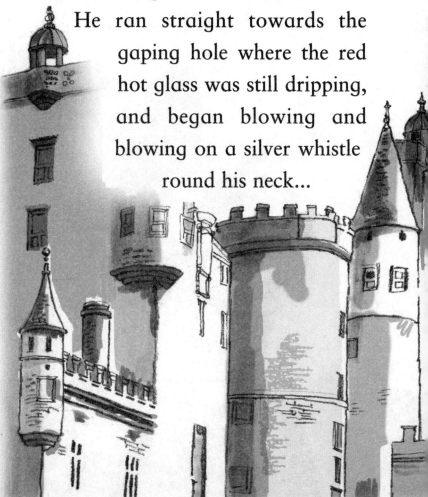

...and the dragon stopped in mid-air, and hovered there, staring in at him!

It was AMAZING!

"DOWN!" King Percival shouted in a voice like a foghorn. "BAD dragon. DOWN! AT ONCE! Argent, go down to earth!"

The enormous dragon blinked, and all of a sudden she didn't look so scary. She circled, and then dropped down and down until she was out of sight. A moment later she was gone, and only the smell of smoke was left hanging in the air. That, and the little dragon crouched outside on the flat roof. He was squeaking miserably as he called for his mother.

King Percival mopped his forehead as he turned to where we were all standing with our eyes totally popping out of our heads.

"HA!" he said. "Everyone all right? Nobody burnt to cinders?"

I don't think any of us could speak, we were SO surprised by what had happened...but it was strange. Although the dragon had been so gigantic and totally extraordinary, there was something about the way she'd looked at King P that reminded me of the way my dog looked when he knew he'd been naughty. Somehow I didn't feel scared any more. Not at all!

"Good. Good. Glad to hear it. Er...sorry if Argent popped up a bit suddenly. A bit worried about her baby, I expect. Quite understandable, really. We'll fetch

the little fellow in, and take him
back—"

King P suddenly stopped. He
stared, and so did we.

The little dragon had crept
away to the very end of the roof,
and was balanced on the top of a
tall chimney.

"Oh, NO!" Alice whispered. "How ever did he get there?"

"Must have scrambled up somehow," King P said. "He can't fly yet. Might have been looking for soot. He's always hungry."

He went to what used to be the window, and peered out. "Come along, little fella!" he called. "Down you come! Come along!"

But the little dragon wouldn't move. King P called and whistled, but he wouldn't budge.

"Can't his mother to fly up and get him, Your Majesty?" Charlotte suggested.

King P shook his head. "Can't

risk it, m'dear. She's a good old dragon – one of the best – but she's clumsy. She'd have that chimney pot rolling down the roof with one beat of her wings."

He sighed heavily. "Wish I knew what to do. Never even THOUGHT to bring a bag of coal with me. Heigh ho. Guess I'd better go and ask Fairy G for help. You girls run away. No point staying here."

"Excuse me Your Majesty, but shouldn't we keep watch and make sure the little dragon doesn't move?" Sophia asked.

I was SO glad she'd asked.

I don't think ANY of us wanted to leave him there all on his own.

King P pulled at his beard. "H'm. Might be useful. But NO GOING NEAR THE WINDOW. Understand?"

"Yes, Your Majesty," we chorused.

Chapter Four

We broke up into little groups as King P went puffing off down the stairs. Of course, Katie and Charlotte came hurrying over to where Emily, Alice and Sophia and I were standing.

"Did you EVER imagine we'd have a lesson like this?" Katie asked, her eyes shining.

"NEVER!" I said. "I do SO hope that little dragon will be OK."

"I'm glad of THAT!" Perfecta said spitefully, as she barged up beside us. "Because it's ALL your fault, scaredy cat Daisy! If YOU hadn't frightened that dragon he'd NEVER have run away!"

"That's right," Floreen agreed. "You'll probably be expelled when Queen Gloriana finds out!"

"No, she won't," Emily said. "It wasn't her fault she slipped!"

"I DIDN'T slip," I began, and then I stopped. Emily had been right beside me when Floreen tripped me, and if she hadn't noticed, who else would have? If I explained it would just sound as if I was making up excuses.

"Don't worry, Daisy," Sophia said. "Anyone with any sense could see it was an accident!"

I know she meant it kindly, but I began to feel really dreadful.

Especially when Charlotte said, "We'll tell everyone you didn't MEAN to scare him."

Perfecta smiled her sneery smile. "WE knew you were going to scare him as soon as you rushed at him, didn't we, Floreen?"

Floreen nodded. "Trying to pretend you were brave!"

"Daisy IS brave," Emily said. "It's much braver to do something when you're frightened than when you don't care!"

That made me feel even worse...because I hadn't been frightened. I'd been ANGRY – angry with Perfecta.

And then a totally AWFUL thought hit me. What if Perfecta was right? Had I scared him before Floreen tripped me? I was so muddled I didn't know what to think, and then a huge voice BOOMED from the doorway, and my knees turned to jelly.

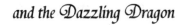

"Could somebody tell me EXACTLY what's been going on in this classroom?"

Fairy G was standing in the doorway, and she was so angry she'd grown to TWICE her usual size. As I put up my hand I was more frightened than I ever could have been of any dragon.

I don't know how I got to the end of my explanation, but I did. Fairy G didn't say anything while I stuttered and mumbled, but I was sure she thought I was terrible. When I'd finished she told me to stay where I was. Everybody else was to go straight to the dining room.

"Please, Fairy G," Katie said bravely, "King Percival asked us to look after the dragon while he got help."

"I will see to that!" Fairy G boomed.

As soon as everyone had gone Fairy G fixed me with a piercing stare.

"Now, Princess Daisy! I'm going to leave you here while I go and see if I can find a sack of coal for poor King Percival. He's tearing his whiskers out with worry about that bad little dragon, but he seems to think it'll come down soon enough if it gets something to eat. And as you tell me it was YOU that scared it away, YOU can wait here and watch it until I get back!"

I noticed Fairy G was more her normal size as she stamped off, and I wondered if I would EVER get used to the way she grew and shrank. I also wondered if I'd totally imagined the very tiny wink I'd seen as she turned round for a moment in the doorway.

Chapter Five

"DAISY!"

I whirled round, and saw Emily, Katie, Alice, Charlotte and Sophia tiptoeing into the room.

"What are you DOING here?" I gasped. "You'll be in SO much trouble if Fairy G finds you! You'll get THOUSANDS of minus tiara points!"

"We couldn't leave you on your own," Alice said. "And we had a BRILLIANT idea! Look! We've brought our fairy cakes! We thought the dragon might be hungry!" And she waved a bag at me.

"I keep telling her he won't like them," Sophia said. "King Percival said he liked coal, but we couldn't find any."

"At least we can try," Alice told her.

I stared at them both. Something was whizzing about in my brain – and then I remembered!!! MY cakes...my

BURNT cakes...WHERE WERE
THEY?

I dashed to my bag, and pulled
it open. YES! They were still
there! And they DID look like
coal!

"LOOK!" I said, and I threw one out of the window. It was much too light to throw very far, and it was a long way from the chimney pot – but the little dragon sat up and LICKED HIS LIPS!

"He LIKES them!" chortled Katie.

"Try and get them nearer," Charlotte suggested.

"Yes," I said. "Yes." And I took a deep breath, picked up my bag, and climbed out of the window and onto the roof.

"DAISY! Come BACK!" Emily yelled. "That's SO DANGEROUS!"

I didn't take any notice. I walked steadily towards the little dragon, and as I got nearer I began to talk to him in a soothing kind of way. When he started to look anxious I stopped, and put two cakes down on the roof tiles.

"There," I said, "there..." Then I walked away just as slowly as I'd come, dropping a trail of burnt crumbs behind me.

I heard the little dragon jump down before I even reached the window, and I could tell by

looking at my friends' faces that he was following me. Katie was beckoning me. Sophia was smiling, and Emily was nodding. Alice and Charlotte were silently clapping. I climbed back into the tower, and trailed more crumbs into the centre of the room until the bag was empty. Then we all

moved right back against the walls, and held our breath.

Pitter patter...pitter patter...and he was INSIDE!

By the time Fairy G came back up the stairs with King Percival, and a page boy carrying a sack of coal, the baby dragon was happily chewing my fairy cakes. I was scratching his ears, and he was purring.

King P looked first amazed, then terribly happy.

"Good boy!" he said, and I thought I could see a tear in his eye. "Oh, WHAT a good boy!"

"Daisy persuaded him to come back," Emily said. "She did it all by herself!"

Fairy G gave me a massive beaming smile. "And I thought you were afraid of dragons!"

"Not any more," I said. And it was true.

And that was the end of our dragon lesson...except for a very very special invitation from King Percival asking all six of us to go to his celebration party!

King Percival
cordially invites you
to a
Celebration Party
Tonight on the roof terrace of his palace
Starts 6:30pm

"I owe you girls a great big thank you," he said in his gruff old voice.

"H'mph!" said Fairy G. She was busy with her wand, repairing the window, but it wasn't a cross kind of "H'mph". "Do they REALLY deserve a treat after all the trouble they've caused?"

"Trouble?" asked King P.

"Tell him, Daisy," Fairy G said, but she was twinkling as she said it.

"It was my fault the baby was scared, Your Majesty," I said. "And I'm TRULY sorry."

"NONSENSE, my dear!" King P shook his head. "Saw it all! You were tripped! Just been telling Fairy G! Saw that Floreen girl stuck out her foot...so I've given her twenty MINUS tiara points. Given you plus points, of course. All six of you. Thirty tiara points each!"

And I'm sure it's VERY unprincessy of me, but I couldn't help being just a LITTLE bit pleased.

Chapter Six

The party was to celebrate the baby dragon's first birthday, and the truly wonderful WONDERFUL thing was that we got to go to King Percival's palace BY FLYING ON A DRAGON! Argent, the baby's mother, was so big that we could all sit on her scaly back, and she flew us all the way.

Oh, it was SUCH fun! The fireworks whooshed and sizzled and banged, and showers of simply beautiful sparkly rainbow stars showered down from the rockets as we danced and danced on the magical rooftop.

When the last firework finally
died away, Argent flew up into
the air and blew fiery smoke rings
that floated gently down to the

ground, and we cheered and cheered. Then the moon came out, and we danced some more in among the silver moonbeams...

...but I don't really remember flying home. I think I was too sleepy.

And I don't know if I dreamt that Fairy G tucked me into bed when we got back, but I'm sure I heard her say, "Good night, Rose Room Princesses! Good night!"

What happens next?
Find out in

Princess Alice

and the Magical Mirror

Hi! I've been LONGING to meet you –
you're the BEST!! Not like horrible Princess
Perfecta, and Princess Floreen. Sometimes
they're SO spiteful! My big sister says it's
because Perfecta didn't get NEARLY enough
tiara points to join the FANTASTIC Tiara
Club last year, so now she's back in the
first year with us. Poor us!

I'm Princess Alice, by the way. I'm
learning to be a Perfect Princess at the
Princess Academy, just like you, but you
know what school is like – HARD WORK!
If it wasn't for Charlotte, Katie, Emily,
Daisy and Sophia, I think I'd COLLAPSE!
And I don't know about you, but I just
can't be good ALL the time...

Check out

website at:

www.tiaraclub.co.uk

You'll find Perfect Princess games and fun things to do, as well as news on the Tiara Club and all your favourite princesses!

Win a Tiara Club
Perfect Princess Prize!

Look for the secret word in mirror writing hidden in a tiara in each of the Tiara Club books. Each book has one word. Put together the six words from books 1 to 6 to make a special Perfect Princess sentence, then send it to us. Each month, we will put the correct entries in a draw and one lucky reader will receive a magical Perfect Princess prize!

Send your Perfect Princess sentence, your name and your address on a postcard to:
THE TIARA CLUB COMPETITION,
Orchard Books, 338 Euston Road,
London, NW1 3BH

Australian readers should write to:
Hachette Children's Books,
Level 17/207 Kent Street, Sydney, NSW 2000.

Only one entry per child.
Final draw: 31 October 2006

The Tiara Club

By Vivian French
Illustrated by Sarah Gibb

All priced at £3.99.

The Tiara Club books are available from all good bookshops,
or can be ordered direct from the publisher:
Orchard Books, PO BOX 29, Douglas IM99 1BQ.
Credit card orders please telephone 01624 836000 or fax 01624 837033
or visit our Internet site: www.wattspub.co.uk
or e-mail: bookshop@enterprise.net for details.

To order please quote title, author, ISBN and your full name and address.
Cheques and postal orders should be made payable to 'Bookpost plc.'
Postage and packing is FREE within the UK
(overseas customers should add £2.00 per book).

Prices and availability are subject to change.